DON'T GET CAUGHT

DRIVING THE SCHOOL BUS

Other books by Todd Strasser

Help! I'm Trapped in a Vampire's Body

Y2K-9: The Dog Who Saved the World

Help! I'm Trapped in a Professional Wrestler's Body

Help! I'm Trapped in My Lunch Lady's Body

Help! I'm Trapped in a Movie Star's Body

Help! I'm Trapped in My Principal's Body

Help! I'm Trapped in My Camp Counselor's Body

Help! I'm Trapped in an Alien's Body

Help! I'm Trapped in Obedience School Again

Help! I'm Trapped in Santa's Body

Help! I'm Trapped in the First Day of Summer Camp

Camp Run-a-Muck series:

#1: Greasy Grimy Gopher Guts

#2: Mutilated Monkey Meat

#3: Chopped Up Little Birdy's Feet

Help! I'm Trapped in My Sister's Body

Help! I'm Trapped in the President's Body

Help! I'm Trapped in My Gym Teacher's Body

Help! I'm Trapped in Obedience School

Help! I'm Trapped in the First Day of School

Help! I'm Trapped in My Teacher's Body

DON'T GET CAUGHT DRIVING THE SCHOOL BUS

TODD STRASSER

AN
APPLE
PAPERBACK

SCHOLASTIC INC.

New York Toronto London Auckland Sydney
Mexico City New Delhi Hong Kong

No part of this publication may be reproduced in whole or in part, or stored in a retrieval system, or transmitted in any form or by any means, electronic, mechanical, photocopying, recording, or otherwise, without written permission of the publisher. For information regarding permission, write to Scholastic Inc., Attention: Permissions Department, 555 Broadway, New York, NY 10012.

ISBN 0-439-21066-6

12 11 10 9 8 7 6 5 4 3 2 1   0 1 2 3 4 5/0

Printed in the U.S.A.   40

First Scholastic printing, November 2000

To Zoe and Max Grodnich

Hey, how's it going? My name's Kyle Brawly and I'm a seventh grader at Hart Marks School. My friends and I call it Hard Marks School, even though it's not that hard. Actually, it's pretty easy. The other thing that's easy to do at Hard Marks is get into trouble.

Believe me, I should know. Does that mean that I'm a troublemaker? Maybe. But you have to understand that at Hard Marks, just about *everyone* is considered a troublemaker.

See, we have this principal, Mr. Chump, who we also call Monkey Breath. He has about six million rules that we're supposed to follow. It's like he doesn't trust us to have any common sense or do anything right on our own.

So it's natural to want to see how many rules you can break without getting caught, right? Let's face it. If you have a choice between doing algebra or trying to bowl a basketball all the way down the hall without it hitting any lockers, which are you going to choose?

(Rule #614: Bouncing, rolling, or otherwise playing with balls in school hallways is strictly forbidden.)

The bizarre thing is, we hardly ever get into trouble outside of school. Because then we have a lot more freedom to do what we want. If it's nice out, we might play some ball or launch a rocket or do some skating. If the weather's crummy, we'll usually hang around inside shooting pool or doing stuff on the computer. It's not like we go around robbing banks or anything.

Anyway, the reason I'm telling you this is to prepare you for this completely weird thing that happened a couple of weeks ago when my friends and I got busted for driving a school bus.

I know what you're probably thinking: *Didn't he say he was only in seventh grade?* Even grown-ups aren't allowed to drive school buses unless they have a special license. But it wasn't like we took the bus for a joyride. Believe me, we had a real life-and-death type reason.

(Not that it wasn't kind of fun. . . .)

But it's a major drag when you try to do the right thing and the whole school winds up hating you for it.

It all started one morning when I met my friend Wilson Kriss at the bus stop.

"You get the call last night?" he asked.

I nodded. "What's Monkey Breath want now?"

Wilson shook his head. "Don't know, but I'm freaked. It's got to be serious when he calls your parents at home and says he wants to see you first thing in the morning, right?"

All I could do was shrug. "We'll find out when we get to school."

Wilson tugged on his earlobe. He does that when he's thinking. He's a mad inventor and definitely one of the most dangerous characters I know. He doesn't look it. He's sort of short and pudgy, and has a round face, rosy cheeks, blond hair, and glasses. Girls think he's cute. Grown-ups think he looks innocent.

It just goes to show you that looks can be deceiving.

"Check this out, Kyle." Wilson took something

out of his backpack. Part of it was one of those old mousetraps with the spring and the bar that's supposed to snap down and break a mouse's neck when it tries to eat the cheese or whatever.

Wilson had glued a thin stick about nine inches long to the side of the bar. And at the end of the stick was a white plastic spoon.

"Let me guess," I said. "A catapult?"

"Nope. A *mouse*apult."

"I get it. So what's the plan?"

"I hate the fruit salad at lunch," Wilson said. At least twice a week they served fruit salad for dessert.

"But it makes great ammunition?" I guessed.

Wilson grinned. "Definitely."

For a moment, both of us pictured the crowded cafeteria. The tables filled with jabbering kids. The lunch monitors yelling at them. From out of nowhere, a single green grape arcs through the air, leaving a thin trail of sticky sweet syrup. It smashes into some kid's forehead and falls into his Lunchable.

The next grape lands in someone's ear.

The next splashes into a cup of tomato soup.

Panic sets in. It's an attack! But from where? Kids run for cover. They retaliate and launch their own grapes. The airspace over the cafeteria is filled with UFFs (Unidentified Flying Fruits). The lunch monitors can't control the crowd. It's an all-out food war!

(Rule #129: Any student caught throwing, playing with, or otherwise using food in an inappropriate way will be severely punished.)

Wilson and I grinned at each other. Suddenly, going to school that day didn't seem so bad, even if Monkey Breath did want to see us.

The smile on Wilson's face didn't last. Coming down the sidewalk toward us were five little kids carrying bright yellow, orange, and blue plastic backpacks. Wilson called them single digits because they were all under ten. I called them the Five Dwarfs. I didn't mind them that much because I have a little brother and I understand that little kids are genetically programmed to be totally annoying. Wilson has a little sister so he should know that, too. But the single digits still gave him fits.

"I hate sharing the bus with them," he muttered.

"We have no choice," I said. "We go to a K-8 school."

"It's gross. Especially Barfy."

Barfy was one of the Five Dwarfs. He had short brown hair, funny glasses with white frames, and a really weak stomach.

Then there was Sneezy, who always had a red,

runny nose and sneezed a lot. Burpy was this cute little red-haired girl who wore dresses and bows in her hair. She looked like a little princess until she opened her mouth and belched. No human being could belch as long and as loud as she could.

We also had Farty. He was skinny and had brown hair that almost fell into his eyes. You didn't have to spend much time with him to realize that his family must have been on an all-bean diet.

Finally, there was Sleepy. She had unruly dirty blond hair, and her clothes were always wrinkled and untucked. You just knew she was one of those kids who never went to bed at night. She was the only kid I'd ever seen actually fall asleep standing up.

The good news was that the dwarfs were completely afraid of us. At the bus stop, they always squeezed together into a little dwarf pod for protection.

The next person to arrive was Amazing Nature Girl. Her real name is Angela Nelson-Gear and some people call her Angie. She has pale skin and stringy brown hair parted in the middle. Amazing Nature Girl is ten and in fourth grade, so technically she isn't a single digit.

Amazing Nature Girl walked right up to us. Unlike the Five Dwarfs, she isn't scared of anyone or anything.

"Did Ms. Taylor like that wasp nest?" she asked.

Wilson and I looked at each other and frowned. The day before, we'd found a wasp nest and put it in a shoe box to bring to school to show Ms. Taylor, our science teacher.

"What did you do with it, Kyle?" Wilson asked me.

"Nothing," I said. "I thought you had it."

"You had it on the bus," he said.

"No, you did," I said.

Amazing Nature Girl stared at us. "You left it on the bus with Grandma?"

"**Y**o, dudes." Before we could answer Amazing Nature Girl, our friend Dusty Lane strolled up to the bus stop. Dusty is thin and tall and has short brown hair. Where Wilson is sort of compact and wound up, Dusty was all loose and laid back. We call him King Calm.

"Anyone get a call from Monkey Breath last night?" Dusty asked in his slow way.

"We both did," I said.

"What'd we do now?" Dusty asked.

"We don't know," said Wilson. "But remember the wasp nest we found? Kyle left it on the bus with Grandma."

"Not me, you," I shot back.

"Don't sweat it," Dusty said with an easy smile. "As long as she didn't open the shoe box, who cares? Anyone collect the bus stop tax yet?"

"Not yet," I said.

Dusty turned to the dwarf pod. "All right, mini-people, time to cough it up."

All the single digits except Sleepy stuck their hands in their pockets and pulled out candy. Sleepy was half asleep and never remembered to bring candy anyway. So Dusty declared her tax-exempt.

The rest of the single digits gave the candy to Dusty.

"What'd we get?" Wilson asked eagerly.

Dusty handed a few pieces to him and a few to me. "Doodly squat. Tootsie Rolls, chocolate kisses, a couple of Now and Laters."

"I can't believe you guys take candy from little kids," Amazing Nature Girl said. "It's so mean."

"Hey, chill out." Dusty unwrapped a Tootsie Roll and slid it into his mouth. "Everybody pays taxes."

"And it's not like we really take *their* candy," I added. "They bring extra for us, so they still get to keep some for themselves."

"Exactly," said Dusty. "If we were really mean, we'd take all the candy. But like Robin Hood and his Merry Men, we only take our fair share."

"Like Robin Hood, do you give it to the poor?" Amazing Nature Girl asked.

"Yes," I said. "We're the poor."

"It is this spirit of cooperation that makes our bus stop what it is," Dusty pronounced with a grand grin.

We heard a squeak of brakes, and the school bus pulled up. Like a bright yellow, orange, and blue creature with five heads and ten legs, the dwarf pod started to move toward the door.

But then stopped.

Something inside the bus was different. A big guy wearing a white T-shirt and blue-and-red tattoos on his arms was sitting in the driver's seat.

"Who's that?" Wilson whispered.

"I don't know," I answered. "But it sure isn't Grandma."

Inside the bus, the new driver pulled on the metal thing that opened the door. Only the door didn't open. He yanked on it again with no luck. Next, he got up and ducked under the bar between the driver's seat and the aisle. He went down the bus steps and pushed on the door. When it still wouldn't open, he stuck his fingers through the black rubber gasket. We watched as he gritted his teeth and strained to make the doors part.

Clank! The door flew open.

"Whoa!" The bus driver waved his arms and caught himself before he fell out of the bus. Standing on the bottom step, he squinted down at us. The skin around his eyes wrinkled. He had broad shoulders and muscular arms and looked a little like that actor in Rambo, only with short hair.

"Well, what are you waiting for?" he snarled. "Get on."

The dwarf pod didn't budge. When anything varied from the normal routine, they got really spooked. Dusty said they were very sensitive to change.

"Where's Grandma?" asked Amazing Nature Girl.

"In the hospital," said the bus driver. "Someone left a shoe box full of wasps on the bus yesterday and she got all stung up."

The thought made me wince. My friends and I shared a guilty look.

"Guess that explains why Monkey Breath called our houses last night," whispered Wilson.

"What's your name?" Dusty asked the new driver.

"Why do you want to know?" the driver asked back suspiciously. I noticed that he didn't talk, he growled. You had to wonder if he'd ever been a gym teacher.

"So we know what to call you," said Dusty.

"You can call me Sarge. *Mister* Sarge."

"Like in the army?" I asked.

"No, like in the state department of corrections," Sarge replied. "That's enough questions. Everyone on board. It's time to go to school."

W e climbed onto the bus. Sarge watched every step we took, as if he expected us to do something wrong.

"Hold it!" He stopped Dusty. "No eating on the bus. Spit it out."

Dusty took his time swallowing the rest of his Tootsie Roll and smiled. "Spit out what?"

Sarge narrowed his eyes angrily, but there was nothing he could do, short of surgery. My friends and I took our usual seats in the back. Not that the back was *that* far back. We had a stubby bus. From the front it looked like a regular school bus, but from the side it was only half as long. As if the company that made it ran out of windows or seats.

The Five Dwarfs always sat near the front. Amazing Nature Girl usually sat in the middle. Sarge closed the bus door, and we started to go. Sneezy raised his hand. "Mr. Bus Driver Man, can we listen to the radio?"

"No, it's against the rules," Sarge snarled as he drove.

(Rule #365: There will be no playing of music, either through radios or on instruments, on the bus.)

Amazing Nature Girl raised her hand next. "How come you stopped driving for the corrections department?"

"None of your business," Sarge snapped. "And no more questions. You're not supposed to talk to the bus driver while he's driving."

(Rule #307: Children are not to disturb the bus driver while the bus is in motion.)

Since Sarge wouldn't let them listen to music or talk to him, the dwarfs quickly got bored. In the front, Barfy got up and crossed the aisle to sit next to Sleepy, who was already asleep with her head against the window and her mouth open.

Without warning, the bus suddenly swerved to the side of the road and stopped so hard that we all slid forward in our seats. At first, I thought we must have hit something. Sarge ducked under the bar and stood in front. He fixed his glare on Barfy. "What did you just do?"

Barfy didn't answer. From the back, we could see that he was trembling with fear. If there was one kid who couldn't handle fear, it was Barfy.

"Well?" Sarge demanded. "I asked you a question."

"Excuse me, Mr. Sarge, sir?" I raised my hand.

"I'm not talking to you," Sarge barked and turned back to Barfy. "Answer me."

The tension was too much. Barfy quickly dug into his backpack and pulled out one of the airplane barf bags his dad always brought home from business trips.

Blarf! Barfy barfed.

Sarge frowned. "What's with him?"

"He barfs a lot," answered Farty.

Barfy neatly folded the top of the barf bag. He placed it on his lap and sat quietly, looking pale.

"Okay." Sarge glared at the rest of us. "Listen up. I don't know what things were like when that old lady drove this bus, but as long as I'm in charge here, we're going to follow the rules. No radio playing. No talking to the bus driver. And most important, no changing seats when the bus is moving. Does everyone understand?"

Amazing Nature Girl raised her hand.

"What?" Sarge growled.

"What subject did you correct?" she asked.

Sarge scowled. "What are you talking about?"

"You said you used to work for the state department of corrections," Amazing Nature Girl said. "So I was wondering what subject you corrected. Or maybe you corrected all of them."

The lines in Sarge's forehead deepened. "The state department of corrections doesn't correct tests. It's in charge of prisoners. I drove a prison bus."

"You mean, like robbers and killers?" Wilson asked, suddenly interested.

"Robbers and killers and worse," answered Sarge. "People who'd done bad things and were in jail for a long time. So don't think I can't handle a bunch of kids like you."

Sarge climbed into the driver's seat, and we started to go again.

"Can you believe it?" I said to my friends. "Sarge used to drive hard-core criminals!"

"Makes sense," Wilson said. "He treats us like we're hard-core criminals, too."

"Think that's why Monkey Breath got him to drive this bus?" Dusty asked.

We started to slow down again. But not because Sarge wanted to yell at us. We'd gotten to Melody Autumn Sunshine's stop. Once again, Sarge had a problem with the door and had to go down the steps and pry it open by hand.

Melody climbed on. She's this really nice, soft-spoken, and friendly person. Her long brown hair is usually braided, and she has a nice smile and always wears lots of colorful beads around her neck and silver rings on her fingers because her parents were hippies. She came down the aisle and sat with us.

"Hey, handsome." She smiled at me.

I felt my face turn hot and knew I was blushing.

"Where's Grandma?" she asked.

"In the hospital," I answered.

"Huh?" Melody frowned.

"Accidental wasp attack," Wilson explained, then opened his backpack. "Check out my latest invention, Melody. I call it the mouseapult."

"Looks dangerous," Melody said.

"Dangerous, huh?" A smile eased its way across Dusty's lips. "Wouldn't this be the perfect place to try it?"

"In the bus?" Wilson asked, surprised. If Grandma had been driving, we never would have tried out the mouseapult. Grandma was really nice. She played the radio for the single digits and she never yelled or lectured us about the rules. If you did something wrong — like you stuck your arm out the window — she just explained why it wasn't a good thing to do and asked you nicely not to do it again. She never had to ask more than once.

But Sarge was a different story.

"What'll we use for ammunition?" I asked.

Dusty reached into his pocket and pulled out a Hershey's kiss from the bus stop tax stash.

"Should work." Wilson placed the chocolate kiss in the spoon. Then he pulled back the metal bar.

"Ready," I whispered, "aim, fire!"

Sproing! The mouseapult released.

Clonk! The Hershey's kiss shot straight up, hit the roof of the bus, and fell on Amazing Nature Girl's head.

"Hey!" Amazing Nature Girl turned and shook her fist at us.

"Sorry!" Wilson called. "Uh, feel free to eat the ammunition."

"A very disappointing first attempt," said Dusty.

"If you're looking for more distance, you may have to reposition the launchpad for a horizontal trajectory," Melody suggested.

Wilson and Dusty gazed at her with awestruck expressions. To hear a *girl* talk like that was just . . . well, amazing. Melody wasn't only really nice and pretty, she was also supersmart. In fact, she was vice president of the student body. No wonder half the guys in the grade had secret crushes on her.

"I'll . . . try that," Wilson stammered.

Dusty dug into his pocket again. "I hate giving up valuable ammunition, but at least it's for a worthy cause."

Wilson reloaded the mouseapult.

"Launchpad repositioned?" I asked.

"Check."

"Fire at will," said Dusty.

Sproing!
The mousetrap snapped closed.
The second Hershey's kiss rocketed forward.
It flew over the heads of the single digits.
And hit Sarge right in the back of the neck.

Sarge slammed on the brakes and steered the bus to the side of the road again. Wilson quickly hid the mouseapult in his backpack. As soon as the bus stopped, Sarge twisted around in his seat, then reached down. He stood up and faced us, holding the Hershey's kiss between his finger and thumb. "Who threw this?"

No one answered.

"There's a rule against throwing objects in a school bus," Sarge said.

"Yeah," Dusty whispered to Wilson and me as if this proved something. "*We* know it. The question is, how does he know it?"

"Sounds like he's *definitely* been talking to Monkey Breath," I whispered.

"We're not going anywhere until whoever threw this raises his hand," Sarge announced.

No one raised his hand. After all, no one actually *threw* the Hershey's kiss. It had been mouseapulted.

"You're all going to be late," Sarge warned.

Dusty winked at me. It didn't take Sarge long to realize that none of us was particularly upset about not getting to school on time. He pressed his lips together and narrowed his eyes angrily. "Okay, listen up. If anything else flies in this bus, you're all going to fly — straight into the principal's office. Understand?"

Sarge sat down and started driving again. Just before we got to school, we went over the railroad tracks and the bus bounced. All the dwarfs except Sleepy and Barfy giggled and laughed because they got to bounce in the air. Sleepy didn't giggle because she was asleep. Barfy didn't laugh because he was too busy holding on to his barf bag so it didn't spill.

We got to school, and Sarge steered the bus into the bus circle. Outside we could see Principal Chump standing on the sidewalk. Our principal is short and shaped like an old-fashioned wooden barrel with legs. His head is more wide than it is long and he has really big ears. He sort of looks like someone who was once six and a half feet tall and was then squashed down to five and a half feet.

Every morning Principal Chump (aka Monkey Breath) stands in the bus circle and yells "No running!"

(Rule #73: Students will not run anywhere on school property unless they are specifically ordered to do so.)

This always puzzles us. Wouldn't Monkey Breath know that the last thing we wanted to do was run to school? If anything, we'd run *away* from it.

Sarge stopped the bus and pulled on the thing that opened the door. This time it opened without a problem. When Grandma was driving, she'd smile and say good-bye to us as we filed out of the bus. But not Sarge. He jumped out and hurried over to Principal Chump.

Still on the bus, my friends and I watched through the window. As Sarge spoke to Monkey Breath, he gestured to the back of his head. We knew he was talking about the flying Hershey's kiss. Monkey Breath turned and stared up at us with a grave expression.

"He thinks we did it," Wilson whispered.

"We *did* do it," I reminded him.

"But he can't prove it." Dusty pulled himself up.

"What about the wasps?" Wilson asked.

"Can't prove that, either," Dusty said. "Come on, don't be nervous. As someone famous once said, 'We have nothing to fear but fear itself.' "

My friends and I got off the bus. Principal Chump was waiting for us. "Anyone know anything about a wasp nest that was left on your bus yesterday?"

We didn't answer. Principal Chump narrowed one eye suspiciously as if he knew there had to be more to the story. You can tell when Monkey Breath wants to look tough and scary. There's just one problem. Those big ears. They're way too big for someone his size, and they sort of stick out. If you gave him a red ball for a nose, he'd look like a clown. This makes it hard to take him seriously.

"There's a rule against bringing dangerous animals on the bus," Monkey Breath said.

I felt like saying that there was a rule against doing almost everything, but it didn't seem worth it.

"There are reasons for rules," Monkey Breath continued. "Without rules there is disorganization. Do you know what happens then?"

My friends and I shook our heads.

"Disorganization invites trouble," our principal said. "Disorganization is the fertilizer that young sinister minds need to create mischief . . . and worse."

"What's worse?" asked Dusty.

Principal Chump's eyes widened. "Worse than mischief? Chaos, evil, lawlessness. The end of civilization as we know it. Do you understand?"

My friends and I nodded.

"Okay, get into school," Monkey Breath said.

We started up the walk and caught up to Melody as we pushed through the front doors and went into school. A big green banner was hanging from the ceiling:

RECYCLE AND WIN!

"What's this about?" Dusty asked Melody.

"The district is having a competition," Melody explained. "If our school wins, we get a free trip to Big Splash Water Park."

"Which means a day off from school!" Wilson realized.

"Sounds good," said Dusty.

I had to agree. Normally, school stuff doesn't hold much interest for my friends and me, but the water park was definitely the bomb. And a day off from school only made it better.

"What do they want us to do?" I asked.

"Collect the most recycling materials, and display them in the most creative way," Melody explained.

Briiiiing! The bell rang. Wilson and Melody hurried toward the school TV station, where he was the chief techie for the daily morning show and she was a roving reporter. Dusty and I headed toward our homeroom. As we went down the hall, Cheech the Leech suddenly appeared in front of us. Cheech comes to school every day wearing the coolest, newest fashion. Baggy pants, skinny pants, long hair, short hair, whatever. He's the kind of kid who attaches himself to you if he thinks you're cool. Because that must mean that he's cool, too. Of course, it doesn't. Everyone knows Cheech wouldn't be cool even if he fell into the Arctic Ocean.

"You going to do it, Kyle?" Cheech asked.

"Do what?"

"The recycling thing."

"I don't know, Cheech. What do you think?"

Cheech always looks kind of stunned when you ask him what he thinks. Basically because he never knows what he thinks. He just wants to think whatever you think.

"I don't know, either," he said. "That's why I asked you."

"Well, I'll let you know," I told him, and went to homeroom.

The rest of the day passed slowly, as usual. At lunch, the stick for the mouseapult broke before Wilson could fire a grape, so the launch was postponed. Later, Sarge drove us home, but in the afternoon the dwarfs were always too tired to be annoying.

The next morning began normally enough. In the kitchen of our town house Mom was blow-drying her hair while she put out bowls for cereal. The news radio was on loud, and the coffeemaker was hissing and gurgling.

The weather forecaster said it was going to be a seasonably cool day.

"How about a light jacket or sweatshirt?" Mom asked.

"It's okay, Mom. I'll be fine."

"Could you get out the milk?"

I went to the fridge and took out a plastic gallon container. It felt awfully light and I could see that there was only about half an inch of milk at the bottom.

"Not much here, Mom."

Mom's eyebrows furrowed and she frowned. "Oh, darn. I meant to stop at the 7-Eleven last night after work. I'm sorry."

Mom works two jobs. During the day, she's a Special Ed teacher over in Jeffersonville where Wilson's cousin Jake Sherman lives. In the evenings and all day Saturday, she waitresses at the Cosmos Diner. It's a pretty hectic life, so you can't blame her if she forgot the milk.

"Don't sweat," I said. "You use it for your coffee. I can have orange juice and toast."

"Undefeated!" My four-year-old brother, Tater Tot, came into the kitchen. His real name is Scott, but I call him Tater Tot because that's his favorite food. He's blond and skinny and for some reason that we don't understand, he likes to pump his fist and shout "Undefeated!"

Tater Tot was wearing a blue South Park sweatshirt inside out and backward, and one black sneaker and one white sneaker.

"Could you fix him up, Kyle?" Mom asked as she shoved some bread into the toaster.

"Over here, Mr. Tot," I said. "And raise your arms."

Tater Tot raised his arms. I pulled off the sweatshirt, turned it right side in, and slid it back down.

"What about those sneakers?" I asked.

Tater Tot looked down. "That's okay."

"No, dude, it's not cool to wear different colors."

"Yes, it is!" Tater Tot insisted. He made a fist and pumped it. "Undefeated!"

"Let him be," Mom said. "As long as he has something on his feet."

The toast came up and Mom buttered it while I poured the uneaten cereal from the bowls back into the box. We never spent more than five minutes eating breakfast. Then it was time for Mom to take Tater Tot to Mrs. Paley's house down the street. Mrs. Paley had three-year-old twins, and she earned extra money by taking care of Tater Tot, too.

Mom went out to the street to start the car. I got my backpack. Tater Tot was standing at the front door, staring at his feet.

"What's wrong?" I asked.

"My sneakers are different colors."

"Mom said it was okay."

"I don't like it," he said.

The front door swung open and Mom came back in. "Come on, I'm going to be late for work."

"He doesn't want to wear two different sneakers," I said.

Mom looked down at Tater Tot, then back out at the car. You could see she was getting frazzled.

"Tell you what," I said to Tater Tot. "You let Mom put you into the car and I'll go find your other sneakers, okay?"

Tater Tot nodded and Mom grabbed him and headed outside. I went into his room and sifted through the toys and picture books until I found his other sneakers. Then I hurried out to the car and handed them through the window to Mom.

"Thanks, Kyle," she said. "It means a lot to me that I can count on you to help and not be a bother."

"No sweat."

When I got down to the bus stop, Wilson and Amazing Nature Girl were already there. The Five Dwarfs were clustered in their bright yellow, orange, and blue dwarf pod. Amazing Nature Girl was telling Wilson about Grandma. "She's still in the hospital."

"How do you know?" Wilson asked.

"She lives behind the Super Stop & Shop. My mom knows her."

"How come she's in the hospital anyway?" I asked. "I've been stung by wasps. It's not *that* bad."

"Turns out she's allergic," Amazing Nature Girl said.

Wilson and I hung our heads and stared at the sidewalk. It was bad enough that we'd accidentally left the nest on the bus and Grandma had gotten stung. Hearing that she was allergic just made us feel worse.

This morning the bus and Dusty arrived at the same time, so he didn't have time to collect the bus stop tax. Once again, the bus door didn't work, and Sarge had to come down the steps and pry it open with his bare hands. This time, he stepped down to the street. The dwarf pod backed away fearfully.

"Yesterday Principal Chump and I had a long talk about the behavior on this bus," Sarge snarled. "We've decided to add some new rules. From now on, we will board the bus in order and by grade. Lower grades first."

"Why?" asked Wilson.

"Because order is the basis for all discipline," Sarge answered. "We've decided to go from youngest to oldest."

"Why not oldest to youngest?" asked Dusty.

"Because you count up, not down," Sarge said.

"What about when they launch rockets?" Wilson asked.

Sarge's eyes bulged a little and you got the feeling he wasn't prepared to discuss it any longer. The dwarfs got on first, then Amazing Nature Girl, then my friends and I. We took our usual seats in the back. Sarge ducked under the bar, got into the driver's seat, and started to drive.

In the front of the bus, Burpy stood up and went to sit next to Sleepy. Sarge jammed on the brakes. The bus veered to the side of the road and lurched to a stop. Our bus driver jumped out of his seat.

"What are you doing?" he shouted at Burpy.

"Sitting," Burpy answered, and smoothed out her skirt.

"Before that," Sarge fumed.

Burpy pointed at the seat across the aisle where Farty was sitting. "I was sitting over there."

"And how did you get from there to here?" Sarge wanted to know.

"I moved," Burpy answered.

"And what did I tell you yesterday about moving?" Sarge asked.

Burpy pointed at Farty. "But he farted."

Sarge rolled his eyes in disbelief. "I don't care who farts or barfs on this bus. *No one moves!*"

Sarge's eyes were bulging and his face was definitely red. He was breathing hard. In the back of the bus, my friends and I shared a puzzled look.

"You get the feeling Sarge is a little high-strung?" I whispered.

"Seems like it," Dusty agreed. "It's kind of strange considering all the criminals he drove around in his old job."

"They were probably in handcuffs and leg chains," Wilson said. "It's pretty obvious he's never dealt with free-range single digits."

My friends and I all grinned. Just at that moment, Sarge happened to look at us.

"You think it's funny?" he growled.

My friends and I had a hard time not telling him the truth, which was that we didn't *just* think it was funny. We thought it was hilarious.

"I would expect you older boys to help instead of sitting there with smirks on your faces," Sarge grumbled.

"How?" asked Wilson.

"Any way you can," Sarge sputtered, then swung under the bar and back into his seat. As the bus started to go, Dusty slowly drummed his fingers against the window.

"What do you think, guys?" he said lazily. "Should we help him?"

"Why?" I asked.

"Well, I think we know whose side he's on," Dusty said with a wink. "So let's find a *creative* way to help, if you know what I mean."

I glanced at Wilson. When it came to creativity, he was The Man. "Any ideas, Mr. Wizard?"

Wilson tugged at his earlobe and thought for a moment. Suddenly, he sat up straight, then leaned over and whispered something into Dusty's ear.

Dusty smiled. "See ya in a bit." He eased himself down between the bus seats and disappeared. Dusty is one of those kids with amazing flexibility. I'd seen him squeeze through windows you couldn't get a basketball through. So crawling under bus seats was a piece of cake.

A little while later his head reappeared under the seat in front of us. He slowly pulled himself up and sat down. The front of his sweatshirt and jeans was covered with a layer of dirt.

"Done." He brushed off his clothes.

A little while later, we arrived at school and got off the bus. But instead of going inside, we stood on the sidewalk and watched through the bus windows while Sarge clapped his hands at the Five Dwarfs and said, "Come on, time to get off. I have other kids to pick up."

What happened next was definitely amusing. The dwarfs started popping up and down in their seats. They wanted to get up, but they kept losing their balance and flopping back down.

In no time, Monkey Breath climbed onto the bus and started yelling. "Come on, let's go. Off the bus!"

The single digits kept popping up and down. They were even starting to develop a rhythm, as if it was a game and they were pretending to be the keys on a player piano. Of course Monkey Breath and Sarge didn't bother to figure out why the dwarfs were popping up and down. They just kept yelling at them to get off the bus.

Finally, through the windows, we saw Principal Chump say something to Sarge. Then Sarge disappeared from view. Standing outside, we could only imagine him crawling down the aisle on his hands and knees.

One by one, the dwarfs popped up and stayed up as Sarge untied their shoelaces from the metal legs of the bus seats. The single digits came down the bus steps and jumped to the ground and hurried toward school. My friends and I held out our hands. As the dwarfs passed us, they slapped our palms. It may have seemed a little corny, but it was our way of letting them know it was all in fun.

It was around the middle of second period when I got called down to the office. Dusty and Wilson were already there, sitting on the bench outside Principal Chump's room. Monkey Breath always makes you wait outside his room for five or ten minutes, just because he thinks it'll make you nervous.

It works a little with Wilson, who tends to be on the nervous side anyway. He was sitting on his hands and tapping his feet rapidly. Dusty's more like me and doesn't mind waiting. He just leans back with his hands behind his head and stretches out his legs.

"Think we're in trouble?" Wilson asked, biting his lip.

"Nothing serious," replied Dusty, King Calm, as if we got called to the office every day. Well . . . that wasn't *that* far from the truth, actually.

After a while, Principal Chump opened his door. "Come in and have a seat, boys."

My friends and I went in. Monkey Breath's office is always perfectly neat. The pens and pencils are lined up on his desk. There's not a speck of dust, not a piece of loose paper anywhere. It seemed a little odd that the curtains on the windows were closed. They made the room dim and shadowy. The only light came from the lamp on the desk.

Since Principal Chump isn't much taller than Dusty or I, he always stands in front of his desk and makes us sit so that he can feel like he's towering over us. The problem when he stands that close is that you can really smell his breath. We don't call him Monkey Breath for nothing.

"You boys are here so often I might as well have chairs with your names on them," he said.

"Cool." Dusty grinned.

Monkey Breath gritted his teeth. "No, Dusty, it is *not* cool. Not by a long shot. When are you boys going to start obeying the rules?"

"We do obey the rules," Dusty said.

"You call tying those little kids' shoelaces to the bus seats following the rules?" Monkey Breath asked.

Dusty nodded.

"How?" asked Monkey Breath.

"Sarge asked us to help keep the dwarfs in their seats," Dusty explained.

"Did he tell you to tie their shoelaces?" Monkey Breath asked.

"He said to do whatever we could," Dusty answered.

"How *else* would we get them to stay in their seats?" I asked.

Monkey Breath ran his fingers through his hair and let out a big sigh. Those sighs were the worst. It was like he was releasing a big cloud of toxic gas from his mouth. My friends and I cringed and tried to cover our noses with our hands without it looking too obvious.

In the bookcase behind Monkey Breath's desk are three thick blue ring binders. Each one has a handwritten title on the spine. One says SCHOOL AND CAFETERIA RULES. The next says RECESS AND PLAYGROUND RULES. The last says BUS AND MIS-CELLANEOUS RULES. Monkey Breath went around behind his desk and pulled the binder titled BUS AND MISCELLANEOUS RULES off the shelf. Then he sat down at his desk and started to thumb through it.

"What's miscellaneous mean?" Wilson asked.

"It's all the stuff that isn't already covered in the other books," Dusty answered.

"Very good, Dusty," Monkey Breath mumbled as he turned the pages of the binder. "Now if only you'd use that brain for learning instead of for figuring out every possible way to break the rules."

"But that wouldn't be any fun," Dusty replied.

Monkey Breath looked up at him. "School isn't supposed to be fun. It's for learning."

"Why can't learning be fun?" I asked.

Monkey Breath blinked, then shook his head and looked back down at the rule book. He thumbed through a few more pages, then pushed a button on his telephone. "Ms. Fortune, would you please come in here?"

The office door opened and Ms. Ivana Fortune came in. She's the assistant principal, and she has red hair and always wears high heels, tight short skirts, big earrings, and bright red lipstick. To my friends and me, Ms. Fortune presents a puzzling philosophical problem: How can an assistant principal also be a babe?

Ms. Fortune took one look at us and turned to Monkey Breath. "Time for a new rule?"

"Yes," replied Monkey Breath.

"Under which heading?" asked Ms. Fortune.

"Bus rules," Monkey Breath said and handed her the BUS AND MISCELLANEOUS RULES binder. "Please add the following: The tying of children's shoelaces to the legs of the bus seats is strictly forbidden."

"Yes, sir." As Ms. Fortune turned to leave, she raised the binder so that it covered the lower part of her face. That way Monkey Breath couldn't see what my friends and I saw — that Ms. Fortune looked like she was about to burst out laughing.

She left and Monkey Breath stood up. "Is there anything you boys would like to say?"

"Yes," said Dusty. "How come the shades are drawn?"

Monkey Breath glanced at the windows and back at us. "People can watch you through uncovered windows."

Out in the main office, the secretaries all smiled as we left. You got the feeling Ms. Fortune had told them about the new rule against tying kids' shoelaces to the bus seats. My friends and I went into the hall and started back toward our classes.

"Monkey Breath is getting seriously weird," said Dusty.

"Believe it," I said. "That thing with the windows is completely whacked."

"Who cares?" Wilson wiped his forehead with relief. "The good news is we got off."

"Dudes, what happened?" Coming down the hall was Cheech the Leech. I wondered how he knew we'd been in the office. Then I remembered that we'd been called down by name over the PA. Cheech was carrying the wooden boys' room pass. He must have timed it so he'd be out in the hall just as we got out of the office.

Dusty winked at Wilson and me and then turned to Cheech. "It's bad, dude."

Cheech's eyes widened. "Really, what?"

"The worst." I bowed my head sadly.

"A week's detention?" Cheech guessed.

"*Way* worse," said Wilson.

"An in-school?" Cheech asked, meaning an in-school suspension.

"Nope."

"A *real* suspension?" Cheech asked in disbelief.

"Worse."

"Expulsion?" Cheech gasped.

"Even worse than that," said Dusty.

"Even . . . worse?" Cheech repeated. "What could be worse than expulsion?"

"Nothing," I answered.

"Huh?" Cheech looked confused.

"Monkey Breath's finally realized that the worst thing he can do to us is nothing," said Dusty.

"Why?"

Wilson, Dusty, and I pretended to look really sad and depressed. "Because if you're not going to get punished, what's the point of doing anything?" I asked.

Cheech blinked. "Oh, yeah. Uh, I get it. You're . . . right. That *is* the worst! Sorry, dudes."

"It's okay, Cheech," Wilson said, hanging his head. "We'll just have to live with it."

The next morning at the bus stop, Amazing Nature Girl told us that Grandma was out of the hospital.

"Is she gonna start driving the bus again?" Wilson asked as he chewed a gummy worm from the school bus tax.

"We'll find out this afternoon," Amazing Nature Girl replied.

"What are you talking about?" Dusty asked.

"Grandma's been our bus driver for a long time," Amazing Nature Girl said. "You know how she always waits if one of us is late. And she lets us listen to the radio and have fun. We owe her a visit."

My friends and I scuffed our shoes against the sidewalk. We knew she was probably right, but who wanted to visit Grandma?

"Suppose we think about it and let you know?" Dusty asked.

Amazing Nature Girl shook her head. "That's

what you always say when you don't want to do something. But I want you to do this. And I'd *hate* to have to tell Principal Chump how the wasps really got on the bus."

Wilson and Dusty stared back at her with looks of pure disbelief. Amazing Nature Girl, a lowly fourth grader, was actually blackmailing us!

And there was nothing we could do about it.

The bus arrived. Sarge had to pry the door open again, and we all climbed on. No sooner did the bus start to move than so did the Five Dwarfs. It was like they were programmed or something. Sarge glanced at the rearview mirror and jammed on the brakes. In a flash, he was out of his seat and standing in the aisle. His face was red, and his eyes were bulging with fury.

"How many times do I have to tell you?" he shouted. "The first and foremost rule! You are *not* to leave your seats!"

The Five Dwarfs looked back at him in silence.

"Don't you kids understand English?" Sarge asked.

Sneezy raised his hand. "Why can't we listen to the radio?"

"I told you, it's against the rules."

I raised my hand. "Excuse me for saying this, Mr. Commander Sarge, sir, but I think it's a question of which rule would you rather have them break? Maybe if you let them listen to the radio they won't move around."

"And maybe you should keep your ideas to yourself," Sarge shot back. "The rules are the rules. You don't break one for the sake of another. If you're interested in suggestions, I suggest you help keep these little kids in their seats."

Sarge sat down hard and started to drive again. The bus lurched forward and everyone's neck jerked back.

Wilson turned to Dusty and me. "Whoa! Talk about a guy who's on the edge."

"You get the feeling that, with just the right amount of encouragement, Sarge might snap?" Dusty asked with an amused smile.

"I wish," I grumbled, stung by the way he'd answered my question.

"And he wishes we'd keep the single digits in their seats," Dusty said, arching an eyebrow.

"Forget it," I replied. "I wouldn't help that guy if . . . wait a minute, what are you suggesting now?"

"Once again, consider whose side he's on," said Dusty.

"Right," I said. Sarge was definitely a student of the Monkey Breath school of discipline.

"So let's help him keep the single digits in their seats," Dusty said in a low voice.

"How?" I asked.

Dusty turned to Wilson. "Got any *new* ideas, Mr. Wizard?"

Wilson *always* has ideas. I'm telling you, the

kid looks like an angel, but he's totally devious. He could probably bring down the whole United States government in a week if he put his mind to it. For Wilson's new plan to work I had to distract Sarge while Wilson and Dusty moved around. I waited until we stopped for Melody, then moved up front and sat down next to Burpy, who was sitting right behind Sarge.

Burpy smiled at me and batted her eyes. I don't know why, but a lot of females do that with me. Even single-digit females.

"Excuse me, Mr. Sarge," I said as we left Melody's stop. "What do you think is wrong with the bus door?"

Sarge gave me a suspicious look in the rearview mirror. "Why do you ask?"

"Just curious."

"Probably needs some oil," he said, and kept driving.

I glanced over my shoulder. In the back of the bus, Dusty and Wilson were on the move from dwarf to dwarf. If they got caught, they'd be busted bad. I had to keep Sarge distracted.

"What's that stick you keep moving?" I pointed at the long metal rod in the floor that Sarge pushed and pulled.

"You know anything about cars?" Sarge asked.

"Not much."

"Well, there's an engine and there are wheels, right?"

"Sure, everyone knows that."

"That stick is the gearshift," Sarge explained. "The gears connect the engine to the wheels. In a car the gears usually shift automatically. But on a bus like this, you have to shift them by hand."

Just like that, Sarge was telling me everything I wanted to know. Some people say I have a special charm. If I do, I don't know how I got it. But I do know that people like to talk to me.

It turned out that Sarge was one of those guys who loved cars. He was more than happy to explain the steering and the gearshift to me. The weird thing was, I was actually interested. I guess because when you're a kid you sit in a car while some grown-up drives and you feel like this is something you could never do. Like steer and press all those pedals and watch out for other cars and people and kids on bikes and junk like that. But now that Sarge explained it all, it didn't seem so incredibly hard.

"How do you know where to shift?" I asked.

"It's designed logically," answered Sarge. "You learn it pretty fast."

I believed him. Little did I know how soon I'd see for myself.

16

For some reason, Principal Chump wasn't waiting in the bus circle that morning. Sarge got out of the driver's seat, ducked under the bar, and faced us. "Okay, I'm glad that you stayed in your seats and obeyed the rules. Everyone off."

My friends and I hurried off the bus, then stood outside and watched. Wilson gave me a nudge and showed me a crumpled tube of Krazy Glue. Inside the bus, the Five Dwarfs leaned forward to get up, but they couldn't. Their plastic backpacks were glued to their seats.

The dwarfs started rocking back and forth as they tried to free their backpacks. Sneezy slipped out of his and tried to yank it from the seat. Sleepy was still asleep.

"Now what?" Sarge yelled. In no time, his eyes got wide and jittery, and he began to look frantic. You definitely got the feeling that he wasn't equipped to handle anything out of the ordinary.

He grabbed the straps of Sneezy's backpack and pulled.

Riiiippppp! The backpack tore in half.

"Whaaaaa! You tore my backpack!" Sneezy started bawling.

"Stop crying!" Sarge yelled frantically. "Just stop it!"

But Sneezy kept sobbing, and that made the other dwarfs cry. Sleepy woke up and started crying, too.

"Oh, man, they're crying." Wilson's shoulders sagged. I guess we all felt bad.

"Just remember, dudes," Dusty said. "Those are basically tears by association. They're not really that upset."

Meanwhile, on the bus, Sarge's eyes darted back and forth and he looked like he didn't know what to do. Outside, Dusty turned to Wilson and me. "Guess we'd better get going."

We'd just started up the walk toward school when a voice yelled, "Wait!"

Sarge was standing on the walk, halfway between us and the bus. Behind him on the bus the Five Dwarfs were still bawling. Sarge looked pale and scared. It was weird, considering he was an adult with muscles and tattoos.

"You can't leave me like this! I've got more kids to pick up and I can't be late. I don't know what you did, but you have to help. *Please!*"

Sarge almost looked like *he* was going to cry. I hate to say it, but I felt kind of bad for the guy.

"Okay," I said. "Give us a second. We'll be right back." I started to lead my friends into school.

"How did Sarge ever handle criminals when he can't even handle single digits?" Dusty asked.

"Good question," I said as we went into the tech shop and grabbed some big green plastic garbage bags. A few moments later we returned to the bus and gave Sarge the bags so that the dwarfs could empty their backpacks into them. Finally, with tear-streaked, red-rimmed eyes, the dwarfs got off the bus, clutching plastic garbage bags with their stuff inside.

Sarge gave us an angry look, then closed the bus door and took off. My last glimpse was of four whole backpacks and Sneezy's torn one still stuck to the empty seats.

Suddenly, I felt a hand clamp down on my shoulder. I turned and found myself staring into the beady eyes of Principal Chump.

"The three of you, to the office immediately," he growled. "Wait for me there."

"I don't know, guys," Wilson said nervously as we went into school. "You think maybe we went too far this time?"

"Could be," Dusty replied, as unruffled as ever. We got to the office. Through the big windows we could see Ms. Fortune talking and laughing with Mr. Gutsy, the gym teacher. Mr. Gutsy is tall and sort of thin. He doesn't have big muscles even though he stays after school almost every day and works out in the gym. But he hardly has an ounce of body fat, either.

Ms. Fortune and Mr. Gutsy were alone in the office. As soon as my friends and I walked in, they stopped talking.

"Catch you later, Ivana," Mr. Gutsy said to Ms. Fortune, and left. My friends and I sat on the bench outside Monkey Breath's room. Ms. Fortune turned to us. She had a big smile on her face, as if Mr. Gutsy had made her really happy.

"What did you do this time?" she asked.

Dusty told her how we'd glued the single digits to their seats. Ms. Fortune put her hand over her mouth and we could see she didn't want us to see her laugh, but there was no mistaking the glint in her eye.

Today Monkey Breath made us wait for a long time. Ten minutes passed, then twenty, then half an hour. The first period ended and kids started to pass by and look in at us through the windows that separate the office from the hall.

Cheech the Leech came by, looking puzzled, as if he didn't understand why we were in the office if Monkey Breath had decided not to punish us anymore. Melody came by. She brushed her long hair out of her face and gave me a worried look, but I winked back to make her think there was nothing to be concerned about.

When the bell for second period rang, I caught Ms. Fortune's eye. "What's taking so long?"

"I think Principal Chump is waiting for your bus driver to finish his other runs and come back," she said.

Wilson and I shared a concerned glance.

"I'm starting to think this could be serious," Wilson whispered with a worried look.

"Don't sweat," Dusty whispered back.

Just then the office door swung open. Principal Chump came in, followed by Sarge. Sarge held his head high and puffed out his chest like a tough guy.

"I think we have something to talk about, boys," Monkey Breath said. "Let's go."

In Monkey Breath's room, my friends and I sat in our regular chairs. Monkey Breath and Sarge stood with their arms crossed, looking at us silently in the dim light. The curtains on the windows were drawn again.

Finally, Monkey Breath said, "Glue."

"On their backpacks," added Sarge.

"And bus seats," said Monkey Breath.

"It worked," Wilson pointed out. "We kept the single digits in their seats."

Monkey Breath turned to the rule books and once again pulled out the binder titled BUS AND MISCELLANEOUS RULES. Together, he and Sarge thumbed through the pages.

Dusty glanced in my direction and rolled his eyes as if to say he seriously doubted they'd find a rule covering the gluing of little kids to their bus seats.

"This one?" Sarge pointed a finger into the binder.

Monkey Breath read it and shook his head. He turned to the next page.

"What about this one?" Sarge asked, pointing again.

Monkey Breath raised a hopeful eyebrow but then pressed his lips together. "No." He turned to another page.

My friends and I watched as Sarge and Principal Chump read down the page. Big smiles suddenly appeared in their faces.

They'd found something.

Monkey Breath looked up from the binder. His eyes practically sparkled in the dim light. "The use of glue, paint, or any other sticky or staining substance is strictly forbidden on school buses."

Sarge grinned triumphantly. "Looks like you boys are nailed."

"But we were only trying to help," argued Wilson.

"Sorry, you used that argument yesterday," Monkey Breath said.

"But Sarge asked us again *today*," I said.

Principal Chump glanced at Sarge. "That's not true, is it?"

"Well . . . " Sarge hesitated. "I, er, *did* ask them to help keep the kids in their seats."

"With glue?" Monkey Breath asked.

"Absolutely not," said Sarge.

"But you didn't tell us we *couldn't* use glue," Dusty pointed out.

Sarge nodded unhappily. Monkey Breath let out a big stink-bomb sigh that almost knocked us out of our chairs. Then he closed the binder. "I must say that I'm *extremely* concerned about you three. You seem to thrive on finding ways to break the rules. What did I tell you just yesterday?"

"That you keep the curtains closed so people can't see you," Dusty said.

"No, about breaking rules," said Monkey Breath.

"It leads to disorganization," I said.

"Correct," said our principal. "And what is disorganization?"

"Cow manure," said Wilson.

"No, *fertilizer*," Monkey Breath corrected him.

"But cow manure *is* fertilizer," Dusty said.

"Not the kind I mean," said Monkey Breath. "I'm talking about the fertilizer in which mischief grows. And mischief leads to chaos, evil, and lawlessness. And it is my job to make sure that does not happen in this school. For your sakes and for the sake of every student in attendance. Therefore, I am going to call your parents and inform them that while you may not have actually broken the rules, you have certainly violated the *spirit* of the rules."

My friends and I were kind of confused when we left the office.

"The *spirit* of the rules?" Wilson said. "What's that?"

"I don't know," I said. "Maybe it's like the spirit of Christmas."

"Doesn't it just kill you?" Dusty asked. "If Monkey Breath can't get us for breaking the rules, he has to get us for breaking the spirit of the rules. I mean, what kind of garbage is that?"

"At least you can't get suspended for it," I reminded him.

Mom had to work late that night, so I didn't see her until the next morning. She was in the kitchen, setting out breakfast, when I came in.

She gave me a sad look. "I spoke to Principal Chump last night."

"All we did was glue the little kids to their seats," I said.

Just the slightest hint of a smile appeared on Mom's lips, but she quickly forced it away.

"It's nothing, Mom," I said. "Principal Chump's a jerk."

"He may be a jerk, but he's also your boss," Mom said. "School is your job. It's the first of many jobs you'll have in life. Sometimes you'll have nice bosses and sometimes you'll have jerky ones. The problem with misbehaving is that you're not hurting Principal Chump. You're only hurting yourself."

And the problem with Mom was that she was usually right. She was smart and she'd had a lot of jobs in her life.

"It's times like this when I wish your dad was still around," she said with a sigh.

"That's okay, Mom, I know what you're saying," I said. "It's not like I'd have to hear it from Dad to know it's true."

Mom smiled a little. "Thank you, Kyle, I appreciate that. Just promise me this will be the last time you'll get into trouble."

"I promise, Mom."

And I swear I meant it.

A little while later, I met my friends at the bus stop. For once, Dusty was there early.

"What'd your mom say?" Wilson asked me.

"Not much." I shrugged. "Just that I should respect Monkey Breath's rules. How about you?"

Wilson's parents absolutely believed that he was perfect and could do no wrong. "My mom's coming to school this morning. She doesn't want anything written on my record. Like some college is gonna see that I glued some single digits to their seats in the seventh grade and decide not to accept me."

"What about you, Dusty?" I asked.

"Grounded next weekend." Dusty hung his head. That wasn't surprising, either. Dusty's father was strict. He had four sons and he really laid down the law.

The bus arrived, and we waited while Sarge struggled to get the door open. When he saw my friends and me, he pressed his lips together into a hard, straight line.

"New rules," he announced. "Rule number one: No one wears their backpack on the bus. From now on, everyone keeps their packs on their laps."

Dusty raised his hand.

"What?" Sarge growled.

"If we're going to keep them on our laps, would it be okay if we called them lap packs instead of backpacks?"

Sarge frowned for a moment as if there must have been some deep hidden meaning in this question. "I don't care what you call them, just don't wear them on the bus. Rule number two: From now on you will board the bus alphabetically. Now line up."

Two minutes later there was still no line, just a bunch of big kids and single digits milling around in confusion.

"What's the problem?" Sarge barked.

Wilson raised his hand. "This is just a guess, Mr. Commander Sarge, sir, but I have a feeling the single digits don't know what alphabetical means."

Sarge stared at the dwarf pod in wonder. "Is that true?"

The dwarf pod quivered nervously, except for Sleepy, who was half asleep.

"It's simple," said Sarge. "You line up in the order of your last names. Names beginning with A go first. B comes next, and so on."

The Five Dwarfs shuffled around. Burpy was first. Then came Farty. Then came Amazing Nature Girl. After her, Sleepy and Sneezy stood side by side.

"Why are you standing like that?" Sarge demanded. "What are your last names?"

"Strone," yawned Sleepy.

"Strong," said Sneezy.

Sarge blinked.

Dusty raised his hand. "It would be Strone first, then Strong."

"Right. I knew that," Sarge mumbled.

Sleepy and Sneezy took their place in line. The last dwarf was Barfy, whose last name was Yuckski. Dusty, Wilson, and I lined up behind him.

"Wait a minute, why are you three at the end?" Sarge asked.

"You said to line up alphabetically," Wilson answered.

"What are your last names?" asked Sarge.

"Zucker," answered Dusty.

"Zwieg," answered Wilson.

"Zygarlowsky," I answered.

Sarge narrowed his eyes suspiciously. "You sure?"

"You think I could make up a name like Zygarlowsky?" I asked.

Sarge thought about it, then shook his head. "Okay, everyone on the bus."

We climbed on. Sarge was about to get into the driver's seat when Farty raised his hand.

"What?" Sarge said.

"Can we listen to the radio?" Farty asked.

Sarge stared at him. "Why do you keep asking me that?"

"Grandma always played it," Farty said.

"Do I look like Grandma?" Sarge asked.

This question sparked a lot of puzzled looks from the Five Dwarfs.

"I told you, it's against the rules," Sarge snapped.

"But Grandma always played it," said Burpy.

"Then she was breaking the rules," said Sarge.

"But we liked it," said Barfy.

In the back, my friends and I shared a glance.

"Looks like the single digits aren't as scared of Sarge as they used to be," Wilson whispered.

"I think they've figured out that his bark is worse than his bite," I whispered back.

"For the last time," Sarge repeated, "on my bus we don't break the rules. And that means no radio."

Sneezy raised his hand.

"Now what?" Sarge barked.

"Why?" asked Sneezy.

"Why what?" Sarge asked back.

"Why don't you play the radio?"

"Because I said so," Sarge said.

"Why?" asked Sneezy.

"I just told you!" Sarge's face was starting to get red. "It's against the rules."

"Why?" Sneezy asked again.

"Why what?" Sarge said.

"Why is it against the rules?"

"Because."

"Because why?"

Sarge stared at the single digits. He looked tired and his shoulders sagged. "I don't know," he admitted.

"My mommy plays the radio in her car," said Burpy.

"So does mine!" said Farty.

"And mine plays DCs!" announced Sneezy.

"You mean CDs," said Burpy.

Sarge shook his head wearily and slipped into the driver's seat. He started the bus. The single digits kept asking why he wouldn't play the radio, but he didn't answer. In the back, my friends and I were shocked. It appeared that our new bus driver had stumbled upon the only way to deal with the Incredibly Annoying Single Digit Repetitive Question Tactic.

And that was with silence.

I am proud to say that these were no ordinary single digits. These were the evilest, most sinister form of single digits known to man. These were Single Digits with Alternatives.

If Sarge wouldn't give them music, they would give him music. So they started to sing:

Row, row, row your boat
Gently down the stream
Throw the teacher overboard
Listen to her scream . . .
Five days later
Floating down the Delaware
Chewing on her underwear
Wish she had another pair . . .
Ten days later
Eaten by a polar bear
And that's how our teacher died . . .
Joy to the world
The teacher's dead

We barbecued her head.
What happened to her body?
We flushed it down the potty.
Round and round it goes
Until it overflows . . .

We watched Sarge's face in the rearview mirror. He steered calmly and stared straight ahead. He seemed to take the singing okay. But it was too early to tell.

Row, row, row your boat
Gently down the stream
Throw the teacher overboard
Listen to her scream . . .

As the single digits started on the next round, you could see the lines around Sarge's eyes start to wrinkle more deeply.

"Dwarf torture begins to take effect," I whispered.

What happened to her body?
We flushed it down the potty.
Round and round it goes
Until it overflows . . .

As the third round began, Sarge started to grip the steering wheel more tightly. His knuckles turned white.

Five days later
Floating down the Delaware
Chewing on her underwear
Wish she had another pair . . .

The skin around Sarge's jaw tightened. He pulled his lips back and bared his clenched teeth. The muscles under his left eye began to twitch.

"He's cracking," Wilson whispered.

Joy to the world
The teacher's dead
We barbecued her head . . .

Sarge's eyes were starting to bulge. He kept blinking as if he was trying to keep his eyeballs from popping out of his skull.

"We're getting close," Dusty whispered.

Row, row, row your boat
Gently down the stream
Throw the teacher overboard
Listen to her scream . . .

Sarge was almost frozen. His eyes were wide and unfocused. He was breathing so hard that his nostrils were flaring in and out. His arms were shaking.

"He's gonna blow!" I whispered.

But Barfy messed everything up.

He blew first.

In the seat in front of us, Barfy doubled over and held his stomach. "I don't feel good," he moaned. "If I don't sit in the front, I get sick."

My friends and I shared a worried look. We hated to interfere with the dwarfs, but this was serious.

Wilson started to wave. "Uh, Mr. Sarge? Commander Bus Driver, sir?"

The sound of Wilson's voice snapped Sarge out of his daze. His eyes went to the rearview mirror. "What?"

"Barfy's going to hurl if he doesn't move to the front," Wilson said.

"No moving!" Sarge yelled.

"But — "

Blarf! Too late. Barfy blew his chunks into his barf bag.

I'm not sure why, but when Barfy barfed it had a calming effect on the other dwarfs. Or maybe they just got bored with singing. The bus grew quiet, and Sarge started to relax. Since there was nothing else to do, I waited until Melody's stop and then got up and sat down next to Burpy, who was sitting behind Sarge.

Burpy smiled up at me and batted her eyes. The little flirt.

"So what's the deal with that pedal?" I asked over Sarge's shoulder.

As soon as he heard my voice, Sarge scanned the rearview mirror to see what Dusty and Wilson were up to this time. But they weren't doing anything.

"Which pedal?" Sarge asked.

"The one you step on each time you shift the gears."

"That's called the clutch," Sarge explained.

I kept asking him questions about the bus, and Sarge kept giving me answers. What really caught me by surprise was when we stopped at a red light and Sarge glanced at his watch and then turned to me and said, "Tell you what. We're running a few minutes early today. Why don't you stay on the bus after the other kids get off and I'll let you sit in the driver's seat?"

We went over the railroad tracks, and all the kids laughed except Barfy, who was too busy holding on to his barf bag. A little while later, we got to school. The dwarfs got off first, then Amazing Nature Girl, and then Wilson and Dusty.

69

"You coming, Kyle?" Wilson asked.

"Not yet," I said.

Wilson and Dusty scowled. "Why not?"

"Sarge and I are in the middle of something." I gave them a wink Sarge couldn't see. They both frowned but got off.

I stayed on and Sarge let me sit in the driver's seat. It was kind of cool to hold the wheel and to move the stick shift around. Meanwhile, Sarge talked about what it was like working for the state department of corrections and driving hard-core criminals.

"It must have been kind of scary," I said.

"Naw, it wasn't so bad," Sarge said. "We always had guards on the bus. And the inside of the bus was constructed like a jail cell on wheels."

"How come you quit?" I asked.

Sarge gave me a surprised look, as if I'd caught him off guard.

"Well, I . . . er, I didn't quit," he said, hardly above a whisper. "I was fired."

"Oh, gee, sorry. Didn't mean to be nosy."

"No, no," said Sarge. "I'm glad you asked. See, I was fired for not obeying the rules."

"Like what?" I asked.

"Pretty much the same rules as on this bus," Sarge said. "I felt bad for the prisoners, so I'd play the radio for them and let them move around while I was driving. Then one day I had to stop short and a prisoner standing in the aisle fell down and hurt his head. They had an investigation and I was fired."

That made me feel kind of bad. "And we've been giving you a really hard time."

Sarge chuckled. "You're just kids. I know deep down you don't mean it."

I didn't see my friends again until third period, when we all got passes to do research in the media center. Not that we really had any research to do. We just wanted to talk. Of course, like everything else at Hard Marks, there was a rule against that.

(Rule #487: There is absolutely no socializing allowed in the media center.)

The way to get around this is fairly simple. You sit at a table as far away from Mr. Hush (the librarian) as possible. Two guys sit with their backs to Mr. Hush and talk. The third guy sits across from them and watches. If Mr. Hush is looking our way, the "spotter" taps a pen or pencil against his head to signal the talkers to stop.

Dusty took the spotter position. Wilson and I sat across from him with our backs to the library.

"What was going on with you and Sarge?" Wilson asked. The other trick is to talk while looking down at a book or piece of paper so it appears like you're studying.

I told them how Sarge got fired for not following the rules on the prison bus.

"So you think that's why he's so strict?" Dusty asked, as if it was starting to make sense.

"I don't know," said Wilson. "Are we really supposed to believe that under that tough bus driver exterior is a heart of gold?"

"Hey, I'm not defending the guy," I said. "But maybe it makes him a little more understandable."

"Is that all you talked about?" Wilson asked.

"He also showed me how to drive the bus," I replied.

"Get real," Dusty scoffed.

"I am," I said. "Remember the other day when I kept him distracted while you guys glued the backpacks? He told me all about driving the bus. It's kind of cool."

Wilson gave me an awed look. "I don't know how you do it, Kyle, but you could probably get the government to tell the truth about Area Fifty-one."

Dusty tapped his pencil against his forehead. Wilson and I quieted down. Mr. Hush came by.

Mr. Hush is tall and thin, and he must shave his head because it's completely bald, even on the sides. He's pretty cool for a librarian. He knows his job is to keep order in the media center, take care of the books, and make sure no one goes where they're not supposed to on the Internet. He never apologizes for being strict or for really caring about doing the job right. And even though he's usually friendly and sometimes even laughs at our jokes, he doesn't try to be our friend. As a result, most of the kids respect him.

"Hey, Mr. Hush," we said.

"Good to see you in here, boys," he said. "But let's have more studying and less discussion."

Mr. Hush moved on. Wilson and I looked back down at our books.

"Did Sarge actually let you drive?" Wilson asked.

"No way," I answered. "He just let me sit in the driver's seat and push the pedals and move the gearshift and stuff. But it was still the bomb."

Dusty looked past Wilson and me. "Someone wants us."

We swiveled around. Amazing Nature Girl had just come into the library. She waved at us and pointed to her wristwatch.

"What's that about?" Wilson asked.

"That we're going to see Grandma after school," I said.

"I can't wait," muttered Wilson.

23

We agreed to meet Amazing Nature Girl behind the Super Stop & Shop. The bus ride home that afternoon took longer than usual because Sarge had problems with the bus door at every stop. He swore he was going to have it checked out by a mechanic to see what was wrong.

Later, my friends and I skateboarded over to the Super Stop & Shop. The apartments behind it were old and made of brick. A rusty, dented car with four flat tires and a smashed windshield was parked on the street. Graffiti were scrawled on the walls and sidewalks, and the smell of cooking wafted from the open windows.

"High-class place," Wilson quipped.

"Look, she's just a bus driver," I said. "What do you expect her to live in? A mansion?"

A few minutes later Amazing Nature Girl rode up the sidewalk on her bicycle.

"Glad you could make it," she said.

"Like we had a choice," Wilson grumbled.

"Come on, it won't be that bad." Amazing Nature Girl led us across the street toward the apartments. She stopped on the sidewalk and got on her bike again.

"Aren't we going in here?" I asked, pointing at the apartment building.

"No way." Amazing Nature Girl started to ride along the sidewalk. My friends and I skateboarded in the street alongside her.

"I thought you said Grandma lives behind the Super Stop & Shop," I said as I skated.

"She does," Amazing Nature Girl said. "*Way* behind it."

We left the block with the apartment building and passed a block of small one-story houses. The houses on the next block were larger, and on the block after that they were even larger. Finally, we got to a block where the houses were practically the size of mansions.

Amazing Nature Girl stopped in front of a really big pink two-story house with a big red door, stained glass windows, and a red tile roof.

"Is this a joke?" Wilson flipped his board into his hands.

"This is where she lives." Amazing Nature Girl walked her bike up the slate path that cut through the bright green lawn.

Back in the street, Dusty, Wilson, and I didn't

move. Amazing Nature Girl frowned at us. "Are you coming or not?"

"Sure," said Dusty. "When you tell us who really lives here."

"I *did* tell you," Amazing Nature Girl insisted. "Come on and see for yourself."

My friends and I followed her up the walk. Amazing Nature Girl stopped at the big red wooden door and put down the kickstand on her bike. Then she pushed a brass button.

Bong! Bong! Bong! From inside came a sound like a gong. We heard footsteps approaching.

"Who is it?" a voice asked.

"Some of the kids from Grandma's bus," Amazing Nature Girl answered.

The door opened and a woman in a light blue maid's outfit welcomed us. "Please come in," she said. "Ms. Urmey will be so happy to see you. She talks about you all the time. She's been very sad since she stopped driving the bus."

Inside the house, the walls were covered with paintings. Big pots of orange, yellow, and blue flowers sat on pedestals in the corners.

"Please come this way," said the maid. She led us down a hall lined with more paintings. I noticed an unexpected scent in the air.

"Smells like a swimming pool," Wilson whispered.

A moment later we stopped in front of a glass sliding door. The glass was fogged, and the smell of chlorine was strong. The maid pulled open the door, and a cloud of warm steam billowed out.

"Please go in," said the maid. "Ms. Urmey is swimming, but I know she'll be very happy to see you."

We stepped through the sliding door and found ourselves standing beside an indoor pool. Above us, the ceiling was almost all glass, and we could see puffy white clouds in the blue sky. Around the pool were huge reddish flowerpots with big leafy green plants the size of small trees. A lady wearing a white bathing cap and a purple bathing suit was swimming in the pool.

"Hi, Grandma!" Amazing Nature Girl called.

The woman in the pool stopped swimming and looked up at us. She blinked with surprise, then waved. "Oh, hello! Just a moment!"

She swam over to the ladder and climbed out. Still dripping with pool water, she pulled on a fluffy white robe. She pulled off the bathing cap and shook out her gray hair.

"How nice of you all to come!" Grandma gave Amazing Nature Girl a hug. Her face was covered with small pink bumps. You got the feeling that a few days earlier they'd been big red bumps.

She turned to me and my friends. "Boys! How wonderful to see you!"

For a second, I thought she might try to hug us, too. Luckily, she didn't. Instead, she invited us to sit with her around a big glass table.

"So how are you?" Amazing Nature Girl asked.

"Oh, much better, thank you," said Grandma. "Those wasps can give you a nasty sting. I still don't understand what that nest was doing on the bus."

Amazing Nature Girl glanced at my friends and me. Dusty and Wilson shrank down in their chairs.

"Ahem." I cleared my throat. "I hate to say it, but that was our fault."

"How?" Grandma asked.

"We were bringing the nest to school to show Ms. Taylor, but we accidentally left it on the bus," I said.

A lot of people would have gotten mad, but Grandma just nodded and even smiled a little. "Oh, that's all right, boys. I know you didn't do it on purpose."

"Can I ask you a personal question?" said Dusty.

"You want to know what a little old bus driver lady is doing in a house like this?" Grandma guessed.

We nodded.

"I keep wondering the same exact thing," Grandma said. "I used to live over in those apartments behind the Stop & Shop. Then one day about six months ago my son picked me up in his car and drove me here. He said this was where I was going to live from now on."

"That's a nice son," I said.

"That's a *rich* son," Grandma corrected me.

It turned out that Grandma's son had been one of those kids who spent every waking second on the computer. He never even finished high school. Instead he started an Internet company. A couple of years later he sold the company and was practically a billionaire at the age of twenty-three.

"How come you kept driving the bus?" Wilson asked.

"That was my job," said Grandma. "It's all I've ever done. What else would I do all day?"

"Then you're planning to go back again?" Amazing Nature Girl asked hopefully.

The lines in Grandma's forehead and around her eyes wrinkled and her lips fell into a frown. "I'm afraid not. They took away my old route. They said they'd give me a new one, but I told them that if I couldn't drive you kids I didn't want to drive at all. I don't want to start over with a bunch of strangers. You kids are like family to me."

"Why'd they take your route away?" asked Amazing Nature Girl.

"Oh, some silly nonsense about you kids being troublemakers," Grandma said with a shake of her head. "I told Principal Chump that none of you had ever been a bother, but he wouldn't listen."

The maid brought in a big silver tray with a pitcher of milk and an excellent assortment of cookies and brownies. Grandma wanted to know how the Five Dwarfs were and what Sarge was like.

Then it was time to leave. Grandma invited us to come back anytime we wanted and said that we could bring our bathing suits, too.

As we were leaving, I remembered something I'd meant to ask her. "Did you ever have any trouble with the bus door?"

"Oh, yes," Grandma answered. "It's very tricky. You have to know just the right way to open it."

"You know how?" Wilson asked.

"Well, of course, dear," said Grandma. "I drove that bus for years."

Back outside, Amazing Nature Girl started to walk her bike down to the sidewalk. My friends and I picked up our boards. No one said a word. It seemed like we were all lost in thought.

"Know what I don't get?" I finally said. "We've never given Grandma any trouble. Why'd Principal Chump want to get rid of her?"

"You guys really don't know?" Amazing Nature Girl asked.

My friends and I shook our heads.

"Did you get in trouble when you tied the little kids' shoelaces to the bus seat legs?" she asked.

"No," I said.

"Did you get in trouble when you glued them to their seats?"

"No."

"Have you *ever* gotten in trouble for all the rules you've broken?" she asked.

"Well, not really," Wilson answered with a shrug.

"I guess you could say that we're pretty good

at getting off on the odd technicality," Dusty added with a slight hint of pride.

"Exactly," Amazing Nature Girl said. "Principal Chump has been trying to catch you guys for years and he can't. The only reason he hired Sarge was because he hoped if he couldn't catch you, Sarge could."

My friends and I shared a shocked look. Our mouths fell open.

"She's right!" Wilson gasped.

"That's so bogus!" I said.

"Imagine how Grandma must feel," said Amazing Nature Girl. "She never did anything wrong and she still lost the job she loves."

"That's it," I said firmly. "I know that Sarge isn't such a bad guy, and he's only a cog in the Monkey Breath Machine, but we're getting rid of him."

"We need a plan," said Dusty. He turned to Wilson. "What do you say, Mr. Wizard?"

Wilson tugged on his earlobe and thought for a moment. Then he raised a finger in the air. "To the supermarket!"

Half an hour later, we left the Super Stop & Shop with two bulging shopping bags. We had a two-liter bottle of soda, black pepper, a big can of baked beans, a strawberry-rhubarb pie, a package of party invitations, and five white breathing masks like painters wear.

"You sure this is going to work?" I asked Wilson.

"No, but it's worth a try," he replied.

The next morning, we handed out invitations for a special bus stop party. The Five Dwarfs got really excited. You know how little kids love a party.

"Remember," we told them just before we got on the bus. "The party is tomorrow morning. Make sure you get here extra early."

The next morning we showed up at the bus stop early to prepare for the party. Wilson briefed us.

"Okay, here's the plan," he said. "Amazing Nature Girl, you have to make sure Farty eats a lot of beans. Dusty, you have to sprinkle some pepper on Sneezy's shoulders. Kyle, you have to get Burpy to drink tons of soda."

"What are you going to do?" Dusty asked.

"I'm going to get Barfy to eat as much strawberry-rhubarb pie as I can," he said. "And take one of these."

He gave Amazing Nature Girl and Dusty a painter's mask. I took two. Dusty wrinkled his nose. "What's that smell?"

"My mom's perfume," Wilson answered. "I put some in each mask."

"Why?" I asked.

"You'll see," Wilson said.

All the dwarfs except Sleepy showed up early for the party. Burpy arrived in a red party dress and wearing red bows in her hair. Every time she finished a cup of soda, I'd pour her another one, and she'd gulp it down like she'd been lost in the desert for a month.

When I looked around, it seemed like my friends were having success with their little kids, too. Farty's face was smeared with beans, and Barfy was on his second piece of pie.

By the time the bus arrived, the little kids' cheeks were puffed out, and they looked like they were ready to explode. Sarge had to force the bus door open again. He stood on the bottom step and stared down at us. He had bags under his eyes and looked as if he'd been up all night.

"Remember, get on alphabetically!" he yelled. "No moving! No *asking* if you can move! No wearing backpacks! No *asking* if you can wear your backpack! No radio! No *asking* if you can listen to the radio! No singing! No *asking* if you can sing! Understand? Don't *do* anything and don't *ask* anything!"

Burpy raised her hand.

Sarge's eyes bulged with disbelief. "*What?*"

"Why?"

"Why what?" Sarge repeated.

"Why can't we do anything or ask anything?"

Sarge went pale and his whole body seemed to jerk uncontrollably. "Just get on the bus." He climbed back up the steps, swung under the bar, slumped into the driver's seat, and stared straight ahead.

We climbed on. Farty was so full of beans, we had to give him a push from behind to get him up the bus steps. Sleepy, who'd arrived at the last moment, staggered up and immediately went to sleep with her head against the window. As we started toward our seats, Barfy gave me a worried look.

"If I sit back there, I'll barf," he said.

"I know," I answered. "But if you sit there today, you may never have to sit there again."

"Really?" Barfy brightened.

"I hope so," I said.

Sarge closed the door and the bus started to go.

Urrrpppp! Burpy burped.

Fweeeep! Farty let a little one go.

Ha-choo! Ha-choo! Sneezy sneezed twice.

My friends and I watched Sarge in the rearview mirror. He looked like he was dealing with it.

Urrrpppp!

Flweeeep!

Ha-choo! Ha-choo!

Sarge's eyes went up to the mirror. He scowled a little and then looked back at the road.

Urrrpppp!

Flweeerp!

Ha-choo! Ha-choo!

Sarge looked in the rearview mirror again. This time he frowned and twitched.

Urrrppppiiit! Burpy's belches were getting longer.

Flaaaaarp! Farty's "releases" were getting louder.

Ha-choo! Ha-choo!Ha-choo! Sneezy sneezed three times.

In the driver's seat, Sarge bit his lip and stared straight ahead. He gripped the steering wheel more tightly.

"I think it's starting to work," Wilson whispered.

Urrrppppiiitah!

Flaaaaarph!

Ha-choo! Ha-choo!Ha-choo!

Sarge's eyes looked glassy, and he didn't blink. He was breathing hard. The muscles under his left eye kept twitching. You got the feeling he was staring ahead, but that he wasn't seeing the road at all.

Urrriiippppaaatah!

Flaaaarrrrupppppp! Farty let a major one go.

Ha-choo! Ha-choo!Ha-choo!

Barfy raised his hand. He was looking slightly green. "Mr. Bus Driver Sarge?"

Sarge was so out of it he didn't even notice.

"Uh, Mr. Bus Driver Sarge, sir?" Barfy said again.

Sarge still didn't answer. Barfy started to dig through his backpack until he came up with a barf bag.

Blarf!

It started to sound like a symphony.

Urrriiippppiiitah!

Flaaaarruuuuppfumph!

Ha-choo! Ha-choo!Ha-choo!

Blarf! Barfy filled his second barf bag.

Urrriiiippppiiiitttahhh!

Flaaaarrrruuuuupoofuuummph!

Ha-choo! Ha-choo!Ha-choo!

Blarf! Barfy filled his third.

In the rearview mirror, we could see that Sarge's eyes were bulging. He was gripping the steering wheel so tightly his knuckles were white. He was breathing so fast and hard he was practically hyperventilating! The veins in his forehead grew fat and pulsed.

But somehow, he managed to hang on.

26

I gave Wilson a worried look. No matter how many annoying, obnoxious, and gross sounds the Five Dwarfs threw at Sarge, he seemed to be toughing it out.

"It's not working," I whispered.

Wilson bit his lip. "No, duh."

"What do we do now?" Dusty asked.

"There's one last chance," Wilson whispered. "Keep your fingers crossed."

The bus stopped to pick up Melody. She got on and instantly pinched her nose. "What's going on in here?" she asked as she sat down next to us. "It smells really bad."

"We're trying to get rid of Sarge," I whispered.

"How?" Melody asked.

Before I could answer, we got to the train crossing.

The bus bounced over the tracks.

The single digits laughed.

Except Sleepy, who was sleeping, and Barfy, who was trying to hold on to his barf bags.

Only it's hard to hold on to *three* barf bags when you have just *two* hands.

"The masks!" Wilson cried.

My friends and I pulled on the perfume-scented painter's masks. I handed one to Melody.

"Oh, Kyle, that's so sweet of you," she said as her warm smile disappeared behind the mask.

Urrriiiipppppiiitahhhhh!

Flaaaarrrruuuupoofuuummphoo! Farty hit a new high.

Ha-choo! Ha-choo!Ha-choo!

Barfy managed to hold on to two bags. The third hit the floor and burst open.

Splash!

Sarge jammed on the brakes. He twisted around in his seat and stared at Barfy's mess on the floor. His nostrils flared as he took a big sniff. His eyes bugged out, and his mouth fell open.

"Oh, no!" He jumped out of his seat, swung under the bar, and came down the aisle, reaching over the dwarfs to pull open their windows.

"Gotta get rid of the smell!" he muttered loudly to himself as he yanked open window after window. "No mop. No water! Gotta — "

Suddenly he stopped and stared at my friends and me with our masks on. His face went from pure panic to solid stone. "You had it all planned! You must think it's funny! You think it's easy to do all this? I'd like to see you drive this bus!"

"Really?" I asked.

"Sure!" Sarge ranted. "Go ahead! Be my guest! I'd like to see you try — "

Awoooo-woooo! From outside came a distant yet strangely familiar sound.

"Doesn't that sound like a train whistle?" Dusty asked.

Clang! Clang! Clang!

"And that sounds like crossing bells," said Wilson.

Through the bus windshield we saw the red crossing lights begin to blink on and off. The long red-and-white striped gates started to come down. Through the back window we saw the other set of flashing crossing gates drop behind us.

And that could only mean one thing.

"We're on the tracks!" Sarge cried. He spun around and practically dove back into the driver's seat.

Clunk! With a loud, sickening thud, his head smacked into the bar. A second later, he crumpled to the bus floor.

The bus went silent. Everyone stared at Sarge, who lay motionless in the aisle.

"Sarge bumped his head," Sleepy said with a yawn, then closed her eyes and went back to sleep.

"Guess he forgot about the bar," said Wilson.

Awoooo-woooo! The train whistle snapped us

out of our daze. My friends and I looked around. In front and behind the bus, the gates were down. To our left the train tracks stretched off into the distance. To our right, they disappeared around a bend.

Dusty swallowed loudly. "Houston, I believe we have a problem."

28

Amazing Nature Girl and Melody jumped out of their seats and stepped over Barfy's mess. They kneeled down beside our fallen bus driver.

"Mr. Sarge?" Melody said. "Mr. Sarge, sir?"

He didn't move.

Amazing Nature Girl shook his shoulder. "Mr. Sarge?"

Still nothing. Melody looked back at us with wide, frightened eyes. "What if he doesn't wake up?"

Wilson, Dusty, and I didn't have an answer. I think we were still in semishock.

Awoooo-woooo! Everyone looked through the windows. The whistle seemed to come from the right, where the tracks curved away around the bend. We couldn't see the train, but we could hear it.

"Everyone off the bus!" Dusty shouted.

We grabbed the single digits and ran to the front.

"We'll get the little kids off first, then we'll pull Sarge off!" I cried.

Wilson was the first down the steps. He tried to pull the door open. "It won't budge!"

Dusty yanked on the thing that was supposed to open the door. "I can't make it open!" he grunted.

Clang! Clang! Clang! Outside, the crossing gates had come all the way down.

Awooooo! Wooooooo! The train whistle was louder. We couldn't see the train, but we knew it was getting closer!

"Push on the door!" Melody cried.

Wilson pushed as hard as he could. "It still won't open!"

Dusty climbed down, and he and Wilson pushed together.

"It's no use!" Wilson yelled.

"Kyle!" Dusty looked back up the steps at me. "You have to move the bus!"

"Me?" I said.

"You're the only one who knows how to drive," cried Wilson.

"But — "

"You heard what Sarge said!" Dusty yelled. "He'd like to see you try."

"Come on, Kyle!" Melody balled her hands into fists. "You're our only hope."

"But I've never actually driven," I said. "I just talked about it."

"That's more than the rest of us have done," Wilson pointed out.

AWOOOO-WOOOOOO! Just then, the train came barreling around the bend. It was moving fast!

Way too fast to stop!

"Oh, no!" Wilson and Amazing Nature Girl screamed at once.

"Move it, Kyle!" Dusty yelled.

29

I ducked under the bar and climbed into the driver's seat. The engine was still running. I grabbed the steering wheel with one hand. With the other, I pushed on the gearshift.

Screech! A horrible grinding sound came from under the floor.

"What are you doing?" Wilson yelled.

"Trying to make it go!" I yelled back.

AWOOOO-WOOOOOO! The train was growing larger and larger. It was less than fifty yards away!

"Come on!" Melody cried.

Sarge had said something about pushing the clutch when you put it into gear. I stepped down on the clutch and shoved the gearshift.

Suddenly, the bus lurched forward!

"Whoa!" Caught by surprise, everyone in the aisle fell backward like a row of dominoes.

Crash! Pieces of red-and-white crossing gate flew through the air as the bus smashed through it. The next thing I knew, we were bouncing down the road on the other side of the crossing. The bus was going so fast I could hardly hold on to the steering wheel.

"All right!" Dusty cheered as he climbed back to his feet.

"Way to go!" Wilson slapped me on the back.

Melody put her arms around my neck and gave me a hug from behind. "That was great, Kyle. You saved us."

"Now we can stop," said Wilson.

Stop?

"Come on, Kyle," Wilson said. "You heard her. Stop."

"I'd . . . I'd really like to," I said as I held on to the wheel and tried to steer.

"Then do it," said Melody.

"Well, uh, Sarge and I only talked about how to go," I tried to explain. "We never actually got to the stopping part."

"What!?" Wilson cried.

The bus was careening down the road. Luckily, there weren't too many cars around.

"Now, come on, Kyle, you know how to stop," Dusty said with amazing calmness. "You use the brakes, dude."

Right! The brakes! I ducked my head down and stared at the pedals coming out of the floor. There were three. The one on the left was the clutch. The one on the right was the gas. That meant —

Ahwoo! Ahwoo! Ahwoo! Woop-woop-woop! A screaming siren burst on behind us.

"What's that?" Wilson gasped.

"Looks like the men in blue, dudes." Dusty pointed back at the rear windows of the bus. "Otherwise known as the police."

I looked into the rearview mirror and saw red-and-blue flashing lights behind us. "What are they doing here?"

"I bet someone saw the bus on the tracks and called them," said Melody.

"This is the police!" a loudspeaker blared from behind us. *"Stop your bus immediately!"*

"Uh-oh, we're in *major* trouble now," Wilson muttered.

"More than you'd think," I replied.

"Why?" Wilson asked.

"Take a look."

Everyone turned and looked through the windshield. Directly ahead of us was an orange-and-white barricade with a big sign that said:

DANGER!
ROAD CLOSED FOR PAVING
FOLLOW DETOUR

31

By the time I hit the brake, it was too late. *"Everyone hold on!"*

CRASH!

When the bus crashed through the barricade, it wasn't as bad as I thought it would be. When we ran over the big red cement mixer, it wasn't as bad as I thought it would be. When we plowed into the mound of gravel, it wasn't as bad as I thought it would be.

But when the bus finally came to a stop, tilting up the side of the gravel mound, and the police caught up to us . . . *that* was as bad as I thought it would be.

I'll spare you the gory details about how the cops climbed on board with their guns drawn and scared us all silly. How the Five Dwarfs started to cry. How they put Dusty, Wilson, and me in handcuffs, but not Amazing Nature Girl or Melody, probably because they were girls. How they got an ambulance to take Sarge to the hospital. And how they took Dusty, Wilson, and me to the police station and called our parents and made them leave work to come and get us.

I hadn't seen my mom cry in a long time. But she cried that night. She told me to go to my room and stay there. After a while there was a knock on the bedroom door.

"Come in," I said, figuring it was Mom.

The door opened and Tater Tot stuck his head in.

"Hey, little dude," I said.

Tater Tot stepped quietly into my room. "Why's Mommy crying?"

"Because I got in trouble," I said.

"On the school bus?" Tater Tot must have overheard something.

"Yeah."

"She has to go to school?" Tater Tot said.

I nodded. Monkey Breath had called and said he wanted Mom and me in his office first thing in the morning.

"Will they teach her to be a better mommy?" Tater Tot asked.

I scowled for a second, then understood what he meant. "No, little dude, she's a fine mommy. She just has to talk to the principal."

"Oh." Tater Tot nodded. Since he was only four, I wasn't sure if he actually knew what a principal was. He headed back toward the door, but just before he left, he turned to me and made a fist. "Undefeated."

I smiled sadly and made a fist back. "Yeah, little dude. Undefeated."

32

The next morning Principal Chump sat behind his desk with his hands folded in front of him, trying to look calm. Ms. Fortune stood off to the side, her bright red lips pressed in a thin straight line. The curtains were drawn, and the room was lit only by the desk lamp. Monkey Breath had our parents stand in the back of the room while my friends and I sat in our regular seats. On the principal's desk was a pile of newspapers. Our local paper was on top. In big black letters, the headline read:

HARD PARKS FOR HART MARKS!
Local Schoolboys Steal Bus and Crash!

Beneath the headline was a photo of my friends and me in handcuffs. In the background you could see the bus tilted up on the big mound of gravel.

"Hard parks?" Wilson whispered. "I don't get it."

"I think they're talking about the bus," I whispered back. "Like it's up on that gravel mound and that's a hard way to park. It's, like, a goof on Hart Marks."

"Yes, Kyle, that is precisely what it is," said Monkey Breath. "A goof on Hart Marks."

He leaned forward and spoke with slow, carefully chosen words. "Even as we sit here, they're laughing at us. The rest of the school district, the county, the state."

He picked up paper after paper. On the front page of each one was the photo of the tilting school bus.

"Wherever this story appears," Monkey Breath continued, "Hart Marks Middle School will be known as the place where those boys stole the school bus."

"But — " Wilson started to say.

"No buts!" Monkey Breath suddenly shouted. His face instantly became red. "You've made a fool of me and a mockery of this school. You have brought us notoriety and dishonor!" He lowered his voice and leaned over the desk toward us. "And the worst of it is, you had it all planned, didn't you?"

My friends and I caught a blast of monkey breath and winced.

"Don't pretend you don't know." Our principal picked up the perfume-scented masks from his desk and dangled them in front of us. "I've already spoken to those children's parents. I know all about the bus stop party. I know what you fed those children."

I heard a sniff and twisted around in my chair. My mom was dabbing her eyes with a tissue.

"You created a distraction," Principal Chump went on. "You knocked out the bus driver. What I don't know is how far you planned to go. Was it just going to be a joyride? Just some childish way of thumbing your nose at authority? Or were you planning something even more evil? Kidnapping, perhaps? Were you going to take those little children and hold them for ransom?"

Monkey Breath settled back into his chair and folded his arms. My friends and I shared looks of utter disbelief. *Kidnapping? Hold them for ransom?*

Behind us our parents started to protest. "That's absurd!" "It's ridiculous!"

"Please, please." Principal Chump held up his hands for silence. "I owe you parents an apology. This is not all the fault of these three depraved boys. It is my fault as well. I failed to keep them from sliding into the bottomless pit of lawlessness and evil. But now that this has happened, their punishment must be swift and sure."

He turned to Ms. Fortune. "Ivana, please take the boys outside and keep an eye on them."

33

I couldn't believe it. We sat on the bench outside Monkey Breath's room and Ms. Fortune sat at her desk watching us while our principal spoke to our parents in private.

"Kidnapping?" I said.

"That's insane," Dusty grumbled.

I turned to Ms. Fortune. "You don't believe this, do you?"

Ms. Fortune sighed. "I honestly don't know what to believe, Kyle. But the evidence against you is pretty strong."

"How can we prove it's wrong?" Wilson asked.

Brrrriiiiinng! The bell rang and school began. We heard footsteps and the sound of voices as kids came down the hall.

Tap, tap. Someone tapped on the window that separated the office from the hallway. I twisted around and found Melody looking through the glass with a sad and worried expression. She mouthed the words, "Is it true?"

I quickly shook my head and mouthed, "No way!"

But Melody didn't look convinced. Her eyes grew watery. She bowed her head and started away down the hall.

"Melody, wait!" I started to get up.

"Sit down, Kyle," said Ms. Fortune.

"But I have to go talk to her," I said.

"Principal Chump wants you to stay right there," Ms. Fortune ordered. "And believe me, this is one time when you'd better do what he says."

I slumped back down and watched through the window as Melody went down the hall. I kept hoping she might look back.

But she didn't.

"The rumors must be flying," Dusty mumbled.

I knew it was dumb, but I couldn't help looking up at the faces of the kids as they passed in the hall. Almost every one of them narrowed his eyes and frowned when he saw us . . . as if they all believed we were kidnappers.

"Talk about being treated like a criminal," Wilson muttered.

Then Cheech the Leech tapped on the glass. You had to figure that if there was one kid who would have thought what we'd done was incredibly cool, it was him.

But Cheech pulled a wrinkled copy of the local paper out of his pocket and pressed it against the glass. He pointed at the photo of us in handcuffs, then made the loser sign with his thumb and forefinger.

"Ouch!" I groaned. "That really hurts."

"Yeah." Dusty nodded sadly. "When you get dissed by Cheech, you've really hit rock bottom."

34

I don't know how long we sat on the bench outside Principal Chump's office. This had to be the worst thing that had ever happened. Monkey Breath was accusing us of trying to kidnap the Five Dwarfs. He was in his room that very moment trying to convince our parents that it was true. Meanwhile, we'd brought shame to Hard Marks. The whole school hated us.

"Uh-oh," Dusty groaned.

"Now what?" I asked.

"What do you think's going on in there?" Dusty nodded at Monkey Breath's door.

"I don't know," I said.

"Let me put it to you this way, partner," said Dusty. "When they suspend you, they call your parents and send a letter home."

"So this must be worse!" Wilson realized.

Dusty nodded his head sadly. "We're looking at expulsion, guys."

Expulsion?

I winced. That meant private school, only there was no way my mom could afford private school. I was pretty sure Dusty's folks couldn't afford it, either.

What other choice did that leave?

We'd probably have to move to another school district. Maybe to Jeffersonville where Wilson's cousins Jake and Jessica Sherman lived.

But moving would be expensive, and that was bad. Not just for me, but for Tater Tot and my mom. Especially my mom, who only did the best she could for me and my brother.

I leaned my elbows on my knees and stared at the floor. I never meant to get in this much trouble. Really. We were just fooling around.

I was so miserable that I didn't even notice when the main office door swung open and a man came in. As he staggered past me, I looked up.

It was Sarge! He was wearing a light green hospital gown that was tied in the back, and on his wrist was a white plastic ID bracelet.

I opened my mouth to say something, but no words came out. Sarge stumbled past my friends and me as if he didn't even notice we were there. Then he reached for the door to Principal Chump's room.

"Wait!" Ms. Fortune called. "Principal Chump is in an important meeting! You can't go in there!"

Too late. Sarge pushed open the door and barged in.

My friends and I craned our necks to see through the open doorway. Inside the room, Monkey Breath's mouth fell open with surprise. "What are you doing here?"

"I quit!" Sarge shouted. "I can't take it any-more!"

"Can't take what?" Monkey Breath asked.

"The bus!" Sarge screamed. "Those kids!"

"*Those* kids?" Monkey Breath pointed through the doorway at my friends and me.

"No, not *them*!" Sarge cried. "The little ones! They're evil, I tell you, pure evil! I've had it! I'm never driving a bus again!"

Everyone stared at him. Suddenly I realized something and jumped up.

"Kyle, sit down!" Ms. Fortune ordered.

But I couldn't. This might be our only chance.

I went into Principal Chump's room.

"What do you want?" Monkey Breath growled.

"Sarge," I said. "What was the last thing you said to me before you hit your head on the bar?"

Sarge blinked. "I don't remember."

"Come on," I urged him. "It was right after Barfy spilled his chunks and you were really upset and you said . . . "

"I . . . I . . . I said I'd like to see you drive the bus," Sarge realized.

"No!" Monkey Breath gasped and jumped up.

"Yes, he did!" Wilson said as he and Dusty joined us. "You can ask Melody."

"I even asked if you were really serious, didn't I?" I said.

Sarge nodded.

"And you said sure," I went on. "You said go ahead! Be my guest!"

"This is ridiculous!" Monkey Breath banged his

fist on his desk. "Regardless of what your bus driver said, you knew you weren't supposed to drive a school bus."

I turned back to Sarge. "Do you remember what happened next?"

"We . . . we heard the train whistle," Sarge mumbled.

"Right," I said. "We were stuck on the train tracks."

"I had to move the bus, fast," recalled Sarge.

"And then what happened?" I asked.

"I don't remember," Sarge said.

"You ran back to the driver's seat, but before you could sit down you smacked your head on the bar," I said.

"I . . . I guess you're right," Sarge admitted.

"No!" Monkey Breath moaned and slumped into his chair.

I turned to Mom and Dusty's and Wilson's parents. "We were stuck on the tracks and the train was coming. I didn't want to drive the bus, but I didn't have a choice."

Dusty's father, Mr. Lane, looked astonished. "You saved everyone. It sounds to me like you're a hero, not a criminal."

"Nooo!" Monkey Breath buried his head in his arms, but our parents ignored him. The next thing we knew, our parents were hugging us with big smiles on their faces. It wasn't fun, but it beat being expelled.

Before we left the office, Wilson's mom called the newspaper and threatened to sue them if they didn't retract the old story and print a new one the next day. Ms. Fortune called the hospital and they came and took Sarge away, the hospital gown flapping behind him.

Dusty's father made Monkey Breath promise that he'd go on the loudspeaker and tell the whole school that we were heroes, not villains. And my friends and I got him to promise that he'd put Grandma back on our bus route.

At midday, when my friends and I came out of the lunch line, everyone in the cafeteria stood up and cheered. Cheech the Leech blocked our path. He held up his notebook and a pen.

"Could I have your autographs?" he asked.

We signed his notebook and went to eat. At the table next to us, Melody looked over and winked at me. Lunch never tasted so good.

*

So that's the story of how we got busted for driving the school bus. I seriously don't recommend that any of you try it. And I wouldn't glue any single digits to their bus seats, either.

If you do want to have some fun, you could try building a mouseapult. Or put a bar of Ivory soap in the microwave for two minutes and see what happens (but make sure you have your parents' permission first!).

If you want to get back at your big brother or sister, crush a clove of garlic into mush, then put the mush inside a balloon and blow it up. Tie the balloon off and hide it somewhere in your sibling's room.

As for my friends and me, we were just happy that Grandma would be driving again and that we weren't going to be expelled. The school may have thought we were heroes, but we knew who the real heroes were. Never underestimate the power of a single digit.

About the Author

Todd Strasser has written many award-winning novels for young and teenage readers. Among his best-known books are *Help! I'm Trapped in Obedience School* and *Help! I'm Trapped in Santa's Body*. His most recent books for Scholastic are *Help! I'm Trapped in My Lunch Lady's Body* and *Help! I'm Trapped in a Professional Wrestler's Body*.

The movie *Next to You*, starring Melissa Joan Hart, was based on his novel *How I Created My Perfect Prom Date*.

Todd speaks frequently at schools about the craft of writing and conducts writing workshops for young people. He and his family live outside New York City with their yellow Labrador retriever, Mac.

You can find out more about Todd and his books at http://www.toddstrasser.com